ACCRINGTON STANLEY Saves Bluebell Wood!

by Joe Boyle
illustrated by Tony Blundell

First published in Great Britain 1993 in Young Lions

Young Lions is an imprint of the Children's Division,
part of HarperCollins Publishers Ltd,
77/85 Fulham Palace Road, Hammersmith,
London W6 8JB

Text copyright © Joe Boyle 1993
Illustrations copyright © Tony Blundell 1993

The author asserts the moral right to be
identified as the author of this work.

ISBN 0 00 674627 6

Printed and bound in Great Britain by
HarperCollins Book Manufacturing, Glasgow

Stanley Gawthorpe lives in
Accrington, a pleasant little
town in the North of England,
with his dog, Fleabag, and
his dad, Herbert, who owns
a tripe shop.

Only Stanley knows about the secret tripe mine in a cave underneath the shop.

Normally, Stanley is very shy, but whenever he eats a little of the secret tripe he becomes...

ACCRINGTON STANLEY! – Hero of the People!

Which is *very* handy.

Chapter One

This is Bluebell Wood, and it's
not hard to guess why they call
it that.

As you can see, it has
thousands and thousands of
bluebells and there are a good
few cloverbells, but absolutely
no doorbells
(due to the
lack of doors).

In Bluebell Wood, the birds
sing in the trees,

the butterflies
flutter by,

the bees hum
in the flowers,

and old folks sit and
eat their sandwiches
on warm, sunny days.

Stanley Gawthorpe and his dog, Fleabag, love Bluebell Wood.

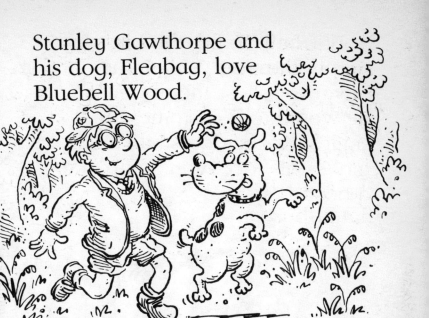

So does Stanley's dad, Herbert. Every day at twelve o'clock, he shuts up his tripe shop and waddles off to Bluebell Wood to eat his lunch (which is always a piece of tripe between two pieces of cake).

And if any of the old folk say "good morning" to him, he always replies "thank you", as he would to a customer, and smiles his squidgy smile that makes his face wrinkle up like a bean bag.

Stanley's dad has been saying "thank you" to his customers for so long, he has forgotten how to say anything else.

Sometimes, Stanley goes to Bluebell Wood to get over his shyness.

He is the shyest boy in the whole world (as well as the untidiest). And if there is a prize to be given for blushing he'd win that, too.

If the prettiest girl in his class,
Betty Blod, smiles at him,

or if his Auntie Flo kisses him,

or if anyone just thanks him for
doing a good deed,
he blushes so much
that his face looks
like a hot water
bottle.

So he comes to Bluebell Wood
and sits against a tree and
listens to the birds singing, the
bees humming, and watches the
butterflies fluttering by, until his
blushes go away.

Fleabag, who is very good at
eating, and not at all shy,
watches the old folks with their
sandwiches, very closely, just
in case they decide to give
him one.

Bluebell Wood is very important to Stanley, to Fleabag, Stanley's dad, Herbert, all the old folk, the birds, the bees, and the butterflies.

Not to mention the bluebells.

Chapter Two

One day, Gravestone Grimshaw, the roughest, toughest kid in the whole of Accrington, caught Stanley, dangled him by his braces from a lamppost, and made him sing

I'M A LITTLE TEAPOT, SHORT AND STOUT.

If Stanley was the shyest and the untidiest boy in the whole world, then Gravestone Grimshaw, with his pointy head, sticky-out ears, piggy nose, broken teeth, and hair that made him look like he'd had an electric shock, was most definitely the ugliest.

Of course, one bite of his secret tripe, and ...FLASH!... plain Stanley Gawthorpe would have become

And then it would have been Gravestone Grimshaw dangling by his braces – but that wouldn't have been fair.

And if there was one thing that Stanley was, it was fair.

After he'd been lifted down by a passing policeman, and ticked off for hanging about, Stanley made his way to Bluebell Wood for a bit of peace and quiet.

15

He didn't get any peace, though it certainly was quiet.

The birds weren't singing.

The bees weren't humming

The butterflies were not fluttering by.

Instead, he found lots of old folk,
and his dad, Herbert, standing
round a big sign, crying.

Stanley looked at the big sign,
and looked at the old folk
crying, and he knew something
was wrong.

The big sign said:

NEW SUPERMARKET
TO BE ERECTED
HERE.

Stanley thought it said:

NO SINGING BIRDS,
NO HUMMING BEES,
NO FLUTTERING BUTTERFLIES,
NO EATING SANDWICHES,
TODAY, THANK YOU.

But that was because he had
trouble reading big words.
And he had always been far too
shy to ask someone to help him.

"Nay, it's nobbut criminal!" said one old lady in her Accrington accent, which, to those who don't live in Accrington, means, *"This is an awful thing to do."*

Stanley felt very, very sorry for the old folk, so he ran off and got them a box of tissues to cry into.

They didn't use the box, but the tissues came in handy.

"Ta, lad," said one old man (meaning, *"Thank you so much, my boy."*)

His dad, Herbert, smiled the littlest smile that Stanley had ever seen him do – so little that it hardly crinkled his face at all.

Stanley could see that the old
folk really needed cheering up,
even though he had no idea
why they were cheered down,
so he popped behind a tree,

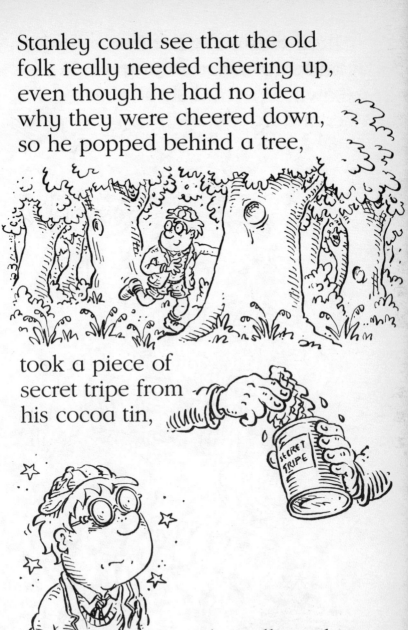

took a piece of
secret tripe from
his cocoa tin,

and swallowed it.

There was a flash, and
suddenly, where Stanley
Gawthorpe had stood one
second ago, was...

He began to do impersonations of singing birds,

humming bees,

and fluttering butterflies (a very difficult impersonation)

just to make the old folk feel better.

The old folk were so grateful they joined in. Most of them impersonated a bird that made a sound like "Booo! Shurrup!"

After an hour of this, one old man was so grateful he offered Stanley his walking stick – in fact he even offered to wrap it round Stanley's neck if he did one more impersonation.

Fleabag wondered why none of them were doing impersonations of throwing sandwiches to dogs.

Then he scratched himself all over, which, apart from eating, was the next best thing he was very good at.

Chapter Three

The next day was Saturday, so Stanley thought he'd go out and see if he could do any good deeds.

Fleabag pricked up his ears. He didn't know what "deeds" were, but if they were good ones they could be tasty.

First of all Stanley had to go to the secret cave underneath the shop to get some more secret tripe.

He had discovered the cave one day when he had tripped over his shoelace and smacked his nose on the fireplace in the little room at the back of the shop.

The fireplace had swung open like a door, revealing the cave with the secret tripe oozing out of the cracks in the walls.

So, off he went to the little back room. He walked up to the fireplace, smacked it with his nose, and sure enough, out it swung, and in he went.

He filled his cocoa tin with the secret tripe, and shoved it in his pocket.

Now for those good deeds!

"Yummy!"
thought Fleabag.

When he got to the High Street, the first thing he saw was a motorcyclist who had accidentally dropped a brick through a jeweller's shop window, and now he was trying to tidy up by shoving the jewellery into a sack.

He seemed to be doing OK so Stanley left him to it.

Over on the other side of the road, high up on a building, another man was entertaining the shoppers by clinging to the gutter by his fingertips.

The man had kicked his ladder away, and was singing a song called "He-ellllpp!" He must have been a very good singer, because lots of people were listening to him.

Stanley listened for a minute or so, but he didn't like the tune very much, so he strolled away.

There didn't seem to be a lot happening in Accrington today, and Stanley began to wonder if he was ever going to find a good deed to do. So far he hadn't seen anything that was worth turning into Accrington Stanley for.

Fleabag, however, had turned into a butcher's shop, and right now the butcher was chasing him down the street with a pork chop in his mouth (Fleabag, not the butcher).

"That your dog?"
asked the butcher.

"Erm..." began Stanley,
"Errrmmm...er..."

And he blushed so much his
face looked like a big, red
balloon.

As Fleabag and the butcher
faded into the distance, Stanley
drew his neck into his shoulders,
and made his way towards
Bluebell Wood to sit against his
tree and wait for his blushes
to go.

On the way, he passed the boating pool and saw a man swimming in it, though why the man had all his clothes on Stanley didn't know.

This man was also singing the "Help!" song, and Stanley just couldn't work out why it was so popular.

The words were so *boring!*

Chapter Four

RUMBLERUMBLERUMBLE

Stanley knew that something strange was going on before he got to Bluebell Wood, because he could hear a lot of noise coming from that direction.

And it wasn't birds singing!

Neither was it bees humming!

Or butterflies fluttering by! (though they make hardly any noise, anyway).

It was the sound of an engine.

A BIG engine.

RUMBLERUMBLE

"Maybe there're some good deeds round here," Stanley said to Fleabag, (who had turned up again).

"I hope so," thought Fleabag, "I'm starving."

When they got there, they saw a crowd of old folk, and Stanley's dad, Herbert, waving umbrellas and handbags and looking just about as angry as a crowd of old folk can get.

RUMBLE RUMBL

They were shouting things in their Accrington accents.

Things like:

"Get tha sen owter 'ere"
(Please go off in another direction)
"'Op it, smart" *(Go away quickly)*
and
"Gi' o'er, y' great Nellie"
(Please stop what you are doing).

RUMBLERUMBLE

The next thing that Stanley saw was a sight that he knew very well indeed.

It had a pointy head, sticky-out ears, a piggy nose, and broken teeth, and it was called Gravestone Grimshaw! He was sitting on a fence and laughing. Well, Gravestone called it laughing – to everyone else it sounded like a rusty can being scraped along a concrete path.

And there, sitting behind the driving wheel of a huge great bulldozer, was the pointy head, sticky-out ears, piggy nose, and broken teeth of Gravestone Grimshaw's dad, Demolition Dan.

Chapter Five

Demolition Dan loved to knock things down, almost as much as his son, Gravestone, loved to dangle people from lampposts and make them sing. And Dan had recently bought this shiny, new yellow bulldozer to make the knocking down easier.

Stanley thought that Dan must
have taken the wrong turning
on his way back from the shiny
new bulldozer shop and that the
old folk were trying to give him
directions back onto the road.

It was obvious that Dan couldn't hear them above the noise of the engine, and Gravestone Grimshaw was sending his dad in totally the wrong direction!

"Go on, Dad, straight ahead," he shouted, and his sticky-out ears flapped like tatty pancakes.